This book belongs to

....

QO **Quarto**
Knows

Quarto is the authority on a wide range of topics.

Quarto educates, entertains and enriches the lives of our readers—enthusiasts and lovers of hands-on living.

www.quartoknows.com

© 2018 Quarto Publishing plc

First published in 2018 by QED Publishing,
an imprint of The Quarto Group.
The Old Brewery, 6 Blundell Street,
London N7 9BH, United Kingdom.
T (0)20 7700 6700 F (0)20 7700 8066
www.QuartoKnows.com

A catalogue record for this book is available from the British Library.

ISBN 978-1-78493-925-0

Based on the original story by A. H. Benjamin and Nick East
Author of adapted text: Katie Woolley
Series Editor: Joyce Bentley
Series Designer: Sarah Peden

Manufactured in Dongguan, China TL102017

9 8 7 6 5 4 3 2 1

FSC
www.fsc.org

MIX
Paper from
responsible sources
FSC® C104723

Mum and Lenny were in the kitchen.

Mum asked Lenny to help.

Not now, Mum! I'm eating.

Too late! It rained and the washing got wet.

Dad and Lenny were in the garden.

Too late! The shop was shut.

Tina asked Lenny to stop the water.
Too late! The bathroom got wet.

Sorry, Tina!

Lenny and Terry were at the shop.

Lenny and Terry were late again.

The family were fed up. Lenny did not help.

We must help Lenny.

He was never on time.
He made everybody wait.

Mum was watching television.

Will you come and play?

15

Dad was reading in the garden.

Lenny was too late to play
at the park.

Park

Tina was in the bathroom.
Lenny could not go in.

Not now, Lenny!
I'm washing.

Tina made Lenny
wait and wait.

Lenny was fed up. Everybody made him wait. He did not like it.

21

The family went to the park.
Lenny was on time!

He was never late again.

Story Words

 bike

 Dad

 eating

 garden

 kitchen

 Lenny

 Mum

 park

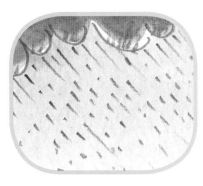 rain

reading

shop

television

Terry

Tina

washing

water

Let's Talk About Not Now, Mum!

Look carefully at the book cover.

Who is on the front of the book?

Can you tell from the character's expressions what they are feeling?

In the story, Lenny is asked to help with everyday tasks.

How do you help around your house?

What jobs do you like doing? Which ones do you not like?

Lenny is always saying "not now".

Why do you think he keeps putting off helping others?

What happens when he doesn't help?

How do you think Lenny feels when he realises what it is like to wait?

Have you ever felt the same way Lenny does?

What lesson do you think Lenny has learnt by the end of the story?

Did you like the story?

Fun and Games

Read the sentences and match
them to the pictures.

1. Tina was in the bathroom.

2. Dad was reading in the garden.

3. The family were fed up.

4. Mum and Lenny were in the kitchen.

Answers: 1:d, 2:b, 3:c, 4:a.

Sound out the letters and read the words. Find the first letter of each word hiding in the picture.

mum   wet   park   shop

29

Your Turn

Now that you have read the story,
have a go at telling it in your own words.
Use the pictures below to help you.

GET TO KNOW READING GEMS

Reading Gems is a series of books that has been written for children who are learning to read. The books have been created in consultation with a literacy specialist.

The books fit into four levels, with each level getting more challenging as a child's confidence and reading ability grows. The simple text and fun illustrations provide gradual, structured practice of reading. Most importantly, these books are good stories that are fun to read!

Level 1 is for children who are taking their first steps into reading. Story themes and subjects are familiar to young children, and there is lots of repetition to build reading confidence.

Level 2 is for children who have taken their first reading steps and are becoming readers. Story themes are still familiar but sentences are a bit longer, as children begin to tackle more challenging vocabulary.

Level 3 is for children who are developing as readers. Stories and subjects are varied, and more descriptive words are introduced.

Level 4 is for readers who are rapidly growing in reading confidence and independence. There is less repetition on the page, broader themes are explored and plot lines straddle multiple pages.

Not Now, Mum! follows a dinosaur boy who does not help his family. It explores the theme of being considerate to others.

Level 2